Check out th
V STECK-VA

Get ready for a
SNA

Is there any truth to the old pirate's poem?
Find out in
FORGOTTEN TREASURE

Are they tough enough to rough it?
Check out the boys who
DON'T LOOK BACK

They're burning rubber in the desert heat!
See who in
ROAD RALLY

Is the big prize worth a big risk?
Get the answer in
VIDEO QUEST

Danger lies where eagles soar. Find out why in
SOARING SUMMER

Knight makes right? See how in
KNIGHT MOVES

The chase is on — but who's hunting who?
Find out, read
DANGEROUS GAME

A family can survive anything, right?
Learn more in
SNOW TREK

ISBN 0-8114-9311-3

8 9 10 07 06 05 04 03

Produced by Mega-Books of New York, Inc.
Design and Art Direction by Michaelis/Carpelis Design Assoc.

Cover illustration: Wayne Alfano

SMOKE

by Alex Simmons

interior illustrations by
Pamela Johnson

STECK-VAUGHN®
C O M P A N Y

CHAPTER ONE

"It smells like a stable in here," Ellie Martinez complained. She was peering into the back of an old pickup truck. The odor of horses, pigs, and chickens was thick. Mr. Dietrich usually used it to cart his livestock around to markets and fairs. Now it was being used to save human lives.

"Just get in, Ellie," Mrs. Martinez urged. Ellie's mother was nervous. "The fire has already destroyed so many homes. Now that it's coming here, we want to make sure you're safe."

A wild forest fire had been burning for days. Flames leaping from tree to tree had ruined acres of forest and property. Anything in the fire's path burned quickly to the ground.

Hundreds of forest rangers and volunteers had been fighting the fire with axes, picks and shovels, water trucks, and even helicopters. But they hadn't been able to stop the raging fire. In fact, they hadn't even slowed it down.

The Martinez house was now the firefighters' command post. Men and

women ran back and forth across the Martinez's lawn. There were forest rangers and state troopers as well as neighbors and local volunteers. All of the firefighters were exhausted and covered with dirt and soot.

Ellie's father helped her into the truck, already filled with other neighborhood children. Then he looked north toward the woods. Ellie followed his gaze.

Clouds of white and gray smoke swept high across the pale blue sky. Just over the tree tops, the smoke was thick and black.

"The wind has shifted again," said Mr. Martinez. "The flames will be here in an hour or two. This is our last chance to save our home."

Ellie started to climb back out of the truck. "Then let me stay and help!"

Mr. Martinez shook his head. "You're too young, Ellie."

"I'm fifteen! Besides, you're letting Hector stay," Ellie protested, "and he's only seventeen."

"Your brother is a volunteer forest ranger," Mrs. Martinez replied. "Besides, he wants to see if Nacho will show up before it's too late."

Nacho was Hector's dog. Nacho had been with the Martinez family since he was a puppy. Ellie knew how much her brother loved that dog.

A white-haired man in overalls came hobbling to the back of the truck. "I've delayed leaving as long as I can," Mr. Dietrich told Ellie's parents. "I've already driven around and picked up all the other children in this area. I've got to get going."

Mr. Martinez quickly kissed Ellie on the cheek. "Adios. We have to get back to work, too. Be safe, sweetheart."

Mrs. Martinez reached up and

stroked her daughter's long black hair. Then Mr. and Mrs. Martinez hurried away to join the other firefighters.

As the truck pulled away, Ellie stared longingly at the Martinez home. Her grandparents had built this house. Her father painted the green trim on the house every year. Her mother tended the garden throughout the seasons. Ellie herself had made the chili-pepper wreath hanging on the front door.

Ellie doubted that her parents had a chance of saving the house. She was sure they were very worried, too.

"I'm glad my grandparents aren't alive to see it go up in smoke," Ellie thought to herself. "It would break their hearts."

Ellie felt like a coward as the truck rocked down the winding road. She'd never run from anything before, not a thing.

"I hate this," she muttered in disgust.

The girl next to her leaned over.

"What's wrong?" the girl asked.

"I should be helping them fight the fire," Ellie said. "It's not like I'm a baby. I'm fifteen years old!"

"I know what you mean," the girl nodded. "My folks made me leave, too."

Ellie leaned against the side of the truck and looked at the other passengers. She recognized some of the children from school.

Ellie spotted one kid she knew very well. The girl's name was Silvia Rivera. She liked being called Silvie. Ellie often baby-sat for the seven-year-old. Silvie was looking out the back of the truck and her eyes were filled with tears.

Ellie leaned over toward her. "It's going to be all right," she said gently. Silvie just looked at her, not saying a word. "They'll stop the fire before it

reaches our homes," Ellie added.

Silvie started to say something, but the truck suddenly jolted to the right. Everyone was thrown about. Ellie heard the brakes screech as they came to a sudden stop.

Ellie and a few other children jumped from the back of the truck to see what had happened. Books, sneakers, pots, pans, clothing, and toys were scattered all over the road in front of them. A big mattress lay in the middle of the heap. On top of it was a broken trunk.

"This stuff must have fallen from someone's truck," said Mr. Dietrich, walking to the front of his truck. He began to drag the trunk off the road.

"Let's help him," Ellie said to the others. The kids began tossing things to the side of the road.

"At least I'm doing something," Ellie thought as she moved a large cardboard box out of the way.

She was gathering up an armful of clothes when something caught her eye. Off in the distance, Silvia Rivera was disappearing into the woods.

A lump of fear suddenly formed in Ellie's throat. Silvie was heading back toward their homes—and straight toward a thousand acres of flames!

CHAPTER TWO

"Stop her!" Ellie cried out.

Mr. Dietrich turned around. "What's going on?" he asked.

"Silvie just ran into the woods!" Ellie answered.

Mr. Dietrich's face turned pale. "Oh, no," he said in a harsh whisper. He took two steps towards the woods then stopped. "I can't leave you all here alone. We've got to get to safety."

"But Silvie's heading back towards the fire," cried one little boy.

Mr. Dietrich hurried back to the truck. "I'll try to call for help on the two-way truck radio."

Ellie ran after Mr. Dietrich and listened to his report.

The speaker on the dashboard crackled a response. "We'll get some people out looking for her as fast as we

can," the ranger replied over the radio. "And we'll try to contact the girl's parents."

"How soon will that be?" Ellie asked Mr. Dietrich.

"As soon as they can," he told her. Then he spoke on the two-way radio again. "I know you're short on help," Mr. Dietrich said. "Just, please, get someone out there soon. Please. Over and out." He turned off the radio.

"Everybody hop back into the truck!" Mr. Dietrich motioned. "We'll be in town in no time," he called to them. "Then I'll hurry back to help look for Silvie."

Ellie climbed into the back of the truck as Mr. Dietrich started up the engine. The truck started down the road to town.

"It'll take a half hour to get to town," Ellie thought. "By then, Silvie could be hurt, or . . ." In a flash, Ellie leaped off the back of the truck. She hit the ground hard and rolled a few feet. Dust flew up around her.

She quickly got up and sprinted toward the woods where Silvie had vanished. Ellie could hear the kids in the truck yelling for her to come back.

She didn't stop.

Ellie leaped over rocks and fallen logs as she ran. Dead leaves and branches crunched under her sneakers.

"This time there is something I can do," Ellie thought.

As she ran deeper into the dense woods, tall leafy trees and dark pines closed in around her. Ellie had always loved the way the sun cut thin shafts of light through the tree tops. She loved the chirping of birds and the smell of pine cones and wildflowers.

But today things were different. The sun's rays were blocked by the billowing smoke and everything was ashen gray. The wind carried the smell of burning

wood. Ellie saw chipmunks, rabbits, and other small creatures racing along the ground looking for safety.

Ellie stopped and called out. "Silvie! Where are you? Come on Silvie, this isn't a game! Where are you?"

No answer.

Ellie continued on. Just ahead of her, she could see a small clearing. She knew this place. The clearing ended at the edge of a rocky cliff. There was a narrow footpath down the side of the cliff, and at the bottom of the cliff was a wide stream with a footbridge. Ellie's grandfather used to take her fishing there. The footpath and stream led to Ellie's house.

Ellie ran as fast as she could, hoping this was the route Silvie had taken.

She was right. As Ellie reached the clearing, she saw Silvie nervously walking along the edge of the cliff. Ellie was relieved to see the girl was all right. She rushed forward.

But Ellie's footsteps startled Silvie. The seven-year-old spun around. Then her eyes went wide. Loose rocks gave way beneath her feet and Silvie began to fall backwards.

Ellie cried out to Silvie as she ran. But she knew she would never reach Silvie in time. The younger girl was going over the edge!

CHAPTER THREE

Ellie made a flying leap for Silvie. She landed on the ground inches from the edge of the cliff. She was just in time—to see Silvie slip from view.

For a second everything seemed too unreal. Ellie felt sick and angry. She closed her eyes. "I almost had you!" she exclaimed.

Then she heard a cry for help. Ellie peered down over the edge.

"Pull me up! Pull me up!" Silvie pleaded. She was hanging a few feet below Ellie. Silvie's hands gripped some roots sticking out from the cliff's side. Her feet dangled in the air. Thirty feet below, sharp rocks jutted out from the ground.

Ellie reached down. Her fingers missed Silvie's hands by an inch. "Reach up with one hand," Ellie coaxed.

"I can't!" the frightened girl replied.

"Hold on and reach!" Ellie ordered. "You've got to try!"

Silvie placed one foot against the cliff wall. As she started to push up, some of the roots she held tore loose. Silvie dropped further.

Ellie lunged down for Silvie, almost going over herself. But she still couldn't reach the young girl.

Suddenly Ellie remembered a rescue story her grandfather had told her. She quickly rose up on her knees. Then she pulled off the leather belt from her blue jeans.

More of the roots tore loose. "Help me, Ellie! Help!" Silvie cried.

Ellie wrapped one end of the belt

around her hand. Then she quickly
lowered it to Silvie. "Grab my belt!" she
shouted.

The last of the roots tore loose the
moment Silvie took hold of the belt. She
clutched the thin leather strap as Ellie

strained to pull her back to the top. With one last giant pull, both girls collapsed safely onto the ground.

"That was a dangerous thing to do," Ellie scolded. She rubbed her sore hands and stood up. "Why were you walking so close to the edge, Silvie?"

Silvie trembled. Her hair was tangled and her face was smeared with dirt. "Why did you come running out of the woods like some wild thing?" she shot back.

"That's what you find in the woods. Wild things," Ellie snapped. "Why did you run away from the truck?" she continued.

Silvie wiped her face on her shirt sleeve. "I have to get back to my house."

"But why?" Ellie asked.

Silvie didn't answer her.

"Stubborn as a mule," Ellie said under her breath. She looked at the sky.

"The fire must be moving closer," she

thought. The sky was getting darker. The stinging odor of burning wood was getting stronger.

Then Ellie heard a helicopter. She jumped up and began yelling and waving her arms in the air. "If we get their attention, they can—"

But before Ellie could finish her sentence, Silvie bolted for the woods.

"What are you doing?" Ellie shouted. She glanced back at the helicopter. Then she ran after Silvie. Ellie caught up with Silvie just a few feet inside the woods.

"What is wrong with you?" Ellie shouted angrily.

"I've got to get back to my house!" Silvie sure was stubborn.

"First, you're going in the wrong direction. Your house is over there." Ellie pointed in a different direction. "And second, what's so important back there?"

"Take me there and I'll show you."

"I'm taking us where it's safe," said Ellie as she took hold of Silvie's arm. "Now let's go."

But Silvie pulled away. "There's something really important at my

house. And if I don't get there soon,
they're all going to die! Please, Ellie,
please. Take me home. I want to go
home!"

CHAPTER FOUR

"What are you talking about?" Ellie asked. "Come on, let's go!"

Silvie refused to budge. "If you try to take me back, I'll just run away again," she said. Tears welled up in her eyes. "Just take me home and I'll show you. Please!" the little girl pleaded.

Ellie glanced off in the distance. The smoke was thick, like a giant wall of black cotton. It seemed to smother even the tallest trees.

"The fire must be moving fast," Ellie thought. If the wind didn't change, they might have just enough time to go to Silvie's house. Besides, Ellie couldn't be sure she could keep Silvie from running away again. That would waste more time. Maybe it was better to just go to the Rivera house and get it over with.

"All right," Ellie said, finally. "But I'm only doing this because your house is close by. Come on. And hurry!"

Ellie quickly led them along a narrow path, then up a steep hillside. In a few minutes the girls were racing towards the Rivera home.

"What's so important that you had to come back here?" Ellie asked as they quickly ran up the brick path to Silvie's front door.

Silvie ran into the house shouting, "Rufus! Here, kitty! Rufus, where are you? Here, kitty, kitty, kitty."

"Your cat?" Ellie asked when she caught up to the younger girl. "You came back here to save your cat?"

"I had to . . ." started Silvie.

Ellie was angry. "Your pet is probably

far, far away from here by now. Cats are a lot smarter than some people."

"But Rufus couldn't leave," Silvie said, running through the house. "She's having kittens!"

"Rufus? *She?*" Silvie was a funny little kid, Ellie told herself. "When is the last time you saw your cat?" Ellie asked.

"Two days ago," Silvie said. She was

becoming more and more upset. "I let her out that morning and I haven't seen her since."

Now Ellie was worried. Rufus might have had her kittens, then hidden them for safety's sake. In that case, finding the animals would take time—and the

girls didn't have much to spare. Through one of the living room windows, Ellie could see the thick black smoke drawing nearer.

"Does Rufus have any special places she likes to go? Does she climb into the kitchen cabinets or crawl behind the furnace?" Ellie asked.

Silvie thought for a moment. "There's the old barn out back," she remembered. "Rufus likes to hunt mice back there."

"Well, come on!" Ellie said. She and Silvie tore out of the house and ran toward the wooden barn out back.

"It feels a lot warmer out here," Silvie said. She looked worried.

Ellie coughed a few times. Her nose and throat felt dry and scratchy. "The fire must be only a few miles away," she said. "We've got to get out of here fast."

The barn looked really old. The boards were all warped and splintered and some had fallen off.

Ellie swung open the large creaking door. It was dark inside. The floor was covered with dust and bits of hay.

Ellie noticed some old wooden crates and some rags over in one corner. She stepped closer. Then she heard several faint meows.

Inside one of the crates, Ellie found five tiny kittens. They were huddled together on top of an old plaid shirt.

"They look so scared," Silvie said as she knelt beside them. "Why would Rufus leave them alone like this?"

"Maybe she went off to find food," said Ellie. She quickly checked to see if the kittens were all right. "Or maybe she got caught out there when the fire started and—" Ellie stopped her thought, seeing the panic in the little girl's eyes.

"Do you think Rufus is dead?" the younger girl asked.

"Any cat with a name like Rufus can take care of herself," Ellie smiled. She bundled the kittens up in the plaid shirt.

"We can't just leave," said Silvie. "What if Rufus comes back?"

Ellie hurried for the door. "I don't know if Rufus is coming back here or not. But I do know that if we don't leave, we'll all be toast. And that includes these kittens."

The minute Ellie and Silvie stepped

out of the barn, they began coughing. A
thin layer of smoke was drifting across
the grounds.

Ellie hurried over to the garden hose
at the side of the house. She put the
kittens down, then tore off a sleeve from

Silvie's cotton shirt and soaked it in water. Then she tore the sleeve in two.

"Do what I do!" she told Silvie. The frightened girl obeyed quickly.

The two girls wrapped the wet cloths around their mouths and noses. Ellie lightly sprinkled water all over the shirt full of kittens. She could hear their fearful meows through the cloth.

Silvie suddenly ran for the back door of the house. "I have something to carry them in!" she shouted. "It's just inside the kitchen."

Silvie returned with her backpack, dumping her school books and supplies on the ground as she ran. "I've always wanted to do that," she laughed.

Ellie smiled and placed the kittens carefully in the backpack. Then she pulled the straps over her shoulder.

"Come on," she said as she started to run. "We'll head towards my house. It's closer than going all the way back through the woods to the road. My parents and the other firefighters should still be there."

Running through the woods was like running through a ghostly nightmare. Sometimes the girls could see the trees as barely more than shadowy shapes.

Their eyes stung and teared from the smoke. Wood hissed and crackled. Embers exploded in the air. The heat was almost unbearable.

"This way, Silvie!" Ellie shouted when they arrived back at the clearing at the top of the cliff. The girls hurried down the cliff path as fast as they could, trying not to stumble and fall. They had just reached the bottom when suddenly their path was cut off—and not by the fire.

A herd of deer was racing towards the girls. Their eyes were wide with panic and fear.

Ellie knew that in a matter of seconds the deer could trample them to death.

CHAPTER FIVE

Ellie quickly grabbed Silvie by the arm. "Run!" She pulled the younger girl behind a nearby tree just as the deer reached them.

The herd split up to go around the tree. Several bumped against it, brushing right up beside the two trembling girls.

Ellie could feel the ground shake. She could feel the power of the deer's own fear as they passed.

Then, within a few seconds, they had vanished into the distance.

Ellie could hear Silvie softly crying. "It's all right now," Ellie said. The kittens meowed and stirred in the pack. "I guess the kittens are all right, too!"

Silvie's voice shook. "I was so scared."

"So was I," Ellie admitted. "If we hadn't—"

A loud cracking sound interrupted Ellie. She looked up. Flames were sweeping across the tops of the trees. Hot embers and ashes began to fall like rain. And directly above them a blazing tree limb was crashing to the ground. "Look out!" Ellie shouted.

Both girls jumped out of the way just in time.

"The grass is catching fire!" Silvie shouted. "Which way do we go?"

"This way!" Ellie pointed to the old footbridge which spanned the wide stream. "The water might slow down the flames."

Ellie and Silvie raced across the bridge and started up a small rise.

The smoke was getting thicker. Ellie and Silvie coughed and rubbed their eyes as they ran. Now and then they could hear the faint sounds of firefighters' chain saws and trees falling.

A helicopter flew somewhere overhead, but the tree tops were too thick, and there was too much smoke to see anything.

Then the girls heard another sound. Faint whimpers came at them through the smoke.

"It sounds like an animal in trouble,"

Silvie said. She stopped to look around.

Ellie was uneasy. "Come on!" She tugged at Silvie's arm.

"Look," Silvie said. She pointed to an old barbed wire fence a few yards away. A sandy colored dog was desperately trying to pull away from the fence.

"It's Nacho!" Ellie cried. She ran towards her brother's dog.

Ellie saw that Nacho's collar was

caught on one of the barbed hooks.

"Easy, Nacho," she said in a soothing voice.

"And you made fun of my cat's name!" Silvie teased.

"Nacho is my brother's dog," Ellie told her. She quickly removed the collar from the dog's neck and looked around. "This is the fastest way," she said. "Now let's get out of here."

The girls took off with Nacho running alongside them.

When the two girls reached a small pond, Ellie removed her cloth mask and waded into the water. "Wet down your hair and your clothes," Ellie told Silvie. She splashed water all over her mask, her clothes, the backpack, and Nacho. "It will give us more protection."

Silvie followed Ellie's lead. The girls put their masks back on and continued through the woods. Nacho stayed close to Ellie, whining and barking.

The heat was getting worse. Ellie knew that the dry leaves crunching under their feet could soon become a bed of flames.

"Are we going to get out of this?"

Silvie asked when they stopped to catch their breaths.

Ellie tried to sound calm. "We'd better. Your folks still owe me for the last time I baby-sat you!"

Silvie laughed, but it was a nervous laugh.

The girls had to move even faster now. Flaming branches were beginning to fall more often. Breathing was getting harder, even through their masks. Sweat poured down the girls'

faces, stinging their eyes almost as much as the smoke. Ellie was tired. Her arms were sore and her legs ached. But she knew she had to get them to safety.

They were nearing the Martinez property, but Ellie was troubled. She didn't hear any chain saws, helicopters, or shouting voices.

"It must be really bad," she told Silvie as they hurried along. "I don't see any volunteers out here cutting down trees."

"Why do they do that?" asked Silvie.

"It's called a fire break," Ellie replied. "If you cut down enough trees, the fire has nowhere to go."

"Maybe all of the people are gone! Maybe there's no one at your house." The little girl was beginning to panic again.

Ellie frowned. "We don't know that yet," she said. "And since we don't have anywhere else to go right now, we might as well find out. Let's go!"

Finally, Ellie, Silvie, Nacho, and the little crying kittens neared the edge of the woods. Through the trees Ellie could just see a large clearing. Her house sat in the middle, surrounded by a low rail fence.

Jeeps and pickup trucks were parked by her front gate and on the road. A few men were running quickly across the clearing towards the house.

Silvie saw the people, too. "They're getting ready to leave! Come on!"

Nacho bolted ahead, running straight for the house.

Ellie and Silvie began stumbling towards the clearing. Just before they reached it, something caught Ellie's eye. A small bundle was attached to one of the trees.

Silvie stopped a few steps ahead of Ellie. "Come on, Ellie! What are you waiting for?"

Through the advancing smoke, Ellie

spotted more of the packages attached
to a number of other trees. It took her
only a few seconds to realize what the
bundles were.

Ellie began to sprint. "Run, Silvie!"
she shouted ahead to the smaller girl.

"They're going to blow up the trees! Run as fast as you can!"

"What?"

"They put dynamite on the trees!" Ellie said. She grabbed Silvie and pulled

her along. "They're going to blow up all these trees! "

The girls ran out of the woods and into the clearing. Silvie stumbled and fell, but Ellie pulled her to her feet and they continued on.

Ellie ripped the cloth from her mouth. If she could only let someone know they were there. "Poppy!" she screamed out for her father. "Poppy!"

Then she felt her feet leave the ground. She heard the explosion, she heard Silvie scream. Then everything went black.

CHAPTER SIX

Ellie lay face down. Her ears rang and hurt from the explosions. But she could still hear the sound of trees crashing to the ground behind her.

Ellie tried to get up, but she felt dizzy and weak. She rolled over on her side and felt the backpack press against her. The kittens didn't make a sound.

"Silvie," Ellie called faintly.

Silvie was laying a few feet away. She moaned and tried to push herself up.

Ellie crawled towards her. "We've got to move away from the trees," Ellie said. "They're falling all around us."

"All right," Silvie gasped. "I'll try."

Ellie barely managed to help Silvie to her feet. They staggered a few yards further before a wave of dizziness swept over Ellie. She felt sick to her stomach. "We've got to keep going," she told

herself. But she didn't know if they could.

Suddenly a pair of strong hands took hold of her. Ellie looked up to see her mother. Her father and brother stood by her side. Nacho was wagging his tail behind them.

"How did you find us?" Ellie asked.

"Nacho brought us," Hector replied.

Ellie glanced at the panting dog. "Thanks, Nacho. I guess we're even now," she smiled.

Ellie's father picked her up in his arms and carried her toward the house.

"Silvie—" Ellie moaned.

"We have her, sis," Hector said gently. "Don't worry." He carried the little girl in his arms.

"My backpack! My backpack!" Silvie was crying.

"Ssh, niña. I'll bring it," Mrs. Martinez said.

They all headed back toward the house. Mr. Martinez lay Ellie down on a blanket in the back of a pickup truck. Hector eased Silvie down next to her. Then Hector went off to look for some medical help.

"How do you two feel?" Mrs. Martinez asked. She had brought out some water and more blankets.

"A little better," Ellie replied. She sipped from a cup of water and passed it to Silvie. The dizziness was beginning to fade away.

"Me, too," Silvie added.

"We sent a message to your parents," Mr. Martinez told Silvie. "Mr. Dietrich had reached them earlier, and they thought they'd find you at your house. They're on their way from there now."

Silvie hung her head. "Are they really mad at me?"

Mr. Martinez squeezed her hand. "I think right now they'll just be glad you're all right," he said. "But they might be mad later. We just got the message ourselves that you two jumped from Mr. Dietrich's truck. That's when we saw Nacho barking for us. Why did you do such a reckless and dangerous thing?"

Ellie and Silvie answered at the same time. "The kittens." Ellie reached for the backpack her mother had put down beside her.

Inside the backpack the five little bodies were still. Then Ellie began to take them out. "They're alive!" she cheered, cradling two of the meowing animals in her arms.

"You went back for kittens?" Mrs. Martinez asked.

"I'll explain later," Ellie said.

Her mother's eyes narrowed. "You most certainly will."

"Ellie saved my life," Silvie told Mr. and Mrs. Martinez. "If she hadn't come after me, I never would have made it."

"I couldn't leave her out there alone," Ellie explained.

Mrs. Martinez smiled. "We understand," she said. Then she held Ellie's hand.

At that moment a ranger came

running up to Mr. Martinez.

"We have a break!" she said with excitement. "We have an effective break! The helicopters are going to drop some chemicals, then we can move in there to try to put the fire out! And we should have medical aid for these girls here any minute now."

Everyone looked exhausted, but somehow happy.

"Is it really over?" Ellie asked her father.

"Only if they can keep the fire contained until it burns out," he replied. "It's still spreading in other areas. But at least we were able to get it under control at this end."

Mrs. Martinez kissed her daughter. "Our home is safe!"

"And so is yours, Silvie," the ranger told her.

"All right!" Silvie cheered.

"I have to go help the other

firefighters," Mr. Martinez said. "You two stay put this time," he said to the girls. They looked sheepish as Mr. Martinez and the ranger left.

Half an hour later, trucks filled with firefighters pulled up to the house. Silvie saw her father jump out of one of the trucks. He brought a cat carrier over to the girls. Inside a cat was complaining in loud meows.

Ellie and Silvie looked at each other.

"Rufus?" Ellie asked.

"Rufus," Silvie nodded.

Silvie hugged Ellie. "Thanks for saving my life," she told her. "You're a pretty good babysitter."

"You think so?" Ellie smiled. "Just wait until your parents get my bill!"